TWISTED

A Collection of Sh... ...
Train Girl, Ag...

KRISTINA RIENZI

INDIGO HAWK GROUP

New Jersey

KRISTINA RIENZI

TWISTED: A Collection of Short Stories

Copyright © 2015 Kristina Rienzi

Book Layout: © 2015 BookDesignTemplates.com
Cover Design: Kari March Designs (www. KariMarch.com)
Author Photograph: Jaime Lynn Photography (www.JaimeLynnPhotography.com)

Publisher's Note: This is a work of fiction. Names, characters, places, and incidents are a product of the author's creative imagination. Locales and public names are sometimes used for atmospheric purposes. Any resemblance to actual people, living or dead, or to businesses, companies, events, institutions, or locales is completely coincidental.

INDIGO HAWK GROUP
PRINTED IN THE UNITED STATES OF AMERICA

Twisted / Kristina Rienzi. – 1st ed.

They who dream by day are cognizant of many things which escape those who dream only by night.

—EDGAR ALLAN POE

Also by KRISTINA RIENZI

Choosing Evil
Luring Shadows
Breaking Evil

TRAIN GIRL

A Short Story

{ONE}

HUNDREDS STORMED THE train the moment it arrived at the station. The anxious crowd barely waited for its screech to a halt before they began their chaotic and mad rush to board. Marley felt like a grain of sand in the sea of passengers as they pushed and squeezed their way through the doors.

Wafts of burnt coffee and tobacco smoke filled Marley's nostrils, the final remnants of commuter love affairs. She looked both ways and decided to go left, only to be further jammed in. As the passengers shuffled down the central aisle, each person searched frantically for a private oasis amid the jungle, even if just a seat.

Marley Walker wasn't searching for anything. She just continued to navigate her way through each car until she found a vacant one in the far rear of the train. A flutter of excitement at the quiet alone time took away her angst. She could finally get some downtime. College was exhausting, as it turned out. She couldn't wait to graduate so she could get a real job, and an apartment, just like her big sister, Jenn.

Marley got comfortable in her seat and then collapsed against the window. The train ride was always too long. If it were up to her, she would be able to get back home to her sister in minutes, not hours. There was no place like home, she thought.

Marley opened the crisp hardcover and her shoulders fell in relaxation. It didn't take long for her to quickly disappear into the latest bestselling mystery novel.

"Hello there, young lady."

The conductor interrupted her mental escape into the fictional world of a serial killer, and she shook slightly. Marley closed the book in haste and looked up. "Yes?"

"I thought this car was empty until I saw the top of your head peeking up above the seat cushion." He chuckled lightly. "Anyhoo, do you have a ticket for me?"

"Oh, right." Stupid me, Marley thought. She began rummaging through her purse until finding the crumpled ticket. She handed it to him. Marley wasn't in the mood for making conversation, and the conductor didn't seem to mind. He just thanked her, smiled, then turned on his heels and left.

She sighed, thankful she was all alone again, exactly the way she liked it. For the next thirty minutes, Marley silently devoured the murder mystery.

When she heard the sliding door to her train car open, she assumed it was the conductor passing through again. In reality, she didn't care who it was and never lifted her head from the deception ensuing on the pages below.

Even when the footsteps increased in volume as they approached her, Marley continued to read. Ignoring others was her way of warding people off in life. She did it all the time, figuring if she didn't acknowledge them, they wouldn't engage or interrupt her, and all would be right in the world.

So when the tall, dark and not-at-all-handsome man sat down right next to her, Marley jumped. It was partly out of shock and partly out of fear. The stranger sitting beside her was dinosaur old. His pale, wrinkled skin was in brazen contrast to his monochromatic black suit ensemble. What struck her as even odder were his sharp eyes. They were the color of coal. She had never seen eyes that color before. Their potency set her on edge.

Wondering why he sat down right next to her, Marley stood and scoured the train car looking for her reason to question him. As they were the only two passengers in the car, her suspicion was quickly confirmed.

"I'm sorry, sir." Marley turned to face him, purposely avoiding his gaze again. She was sure he had some ungodly power to control her mind with his evil, black eyes. She swallowed hard before she spoke again, gathering her courage to confront the stranger. "I don't mean to be rude, but I do like to sit alone when I travel. And as you can see, there are plenty of empty seats around." Marley gestured to the vacant car.

"Yes, but this is the seat that belongs to me," the stranger responded firmly, his expression seeking to trap into another fixed look. "There is no other seat for me."

Marley rolled her eyes, let out a huff and sat down, getting back into her book. She wasn't going to win with this crazy old man. "Whatever."

The stranger broke in on her reading. "I realize you have no idea who I am. But I know who you are, Miss Marley Walker," he said.

Chills crept down her spine like a spider going for a leisurely stroll. She snapped her head in his direction. "How—?"

"It's not important how I know who you are," he interrupted. "What is important is that I do know who you are, Marley." He tapped the space between them. "And, this right here is where I'm meant to sit on our train and absolutely nowhere else."

Marley shook her head in confusion. "You're not making any sense. And you're freaking me out." Then she grabbed her bag, shoved the hardcover novel under her arm and stood abruptly. "I'm changing my seat. So if you don't mind moving aside, I'll be out of your way in just a minute."

The dark stranger snatched her arm, stopping her. "Actually, Marley, I do mind. Now sit down quietly before you cause a scene." He pulled her gently back into her seat, making sure to block her exit with his long, lanky leg.

Marley's mouth fell open in disbelief. She contemplated yelling for help but changed her mind. It wasn't worth the effort. He probably saw her name written somewhere, maybe on the interior of her book. It was possible she had flipped it open. She always marked her novels with her name. No matter, it was just a seat on the train and he could have it.

She leaned against the window again. Let him have it his way, she thought. She fell back into her crime story and decided she wouldn't pay the crazy old man any mind for the rest of the trip.

{TWO}

"**Y**OUR SISTER'S LIFE is in danger," the stranger said.

Marley snapped at the man in black. "Excuse me?"

"It's true. However, you do not and will not believe me."

"Why would I believe you? You don't know anything about me or my sister, or even that I have a sister," Marley huffed.

"I beg to differ, Marley. I knew your name, didn't I?"

"Of course you did." Marley flipped her book open to the inside cover to show the man exactly how he had known her name. She pointed to the inside cover. "See?" But when she looked down, the page was blank. Damn it, she thought. Why hadn't she written her name on the inside cover of her new book yet? It would have explained everything. Now nothing made sense.

He shrugged. "I know many things, Marley. Many, many things. You should listen to me, but unfortunately, I know you won't."

Marley shut the novel, embarrassed. She was entirely out of her realm. She had never experienced anything like this before and wasn't sure how to react. At this point, she wanted nothing more than to get off the train at the next stop, but that didn't make sense either. She still had to get home to her sister.

Marley would have to endure the old man's odd antics for the rest of the ride. She knew he was a wacko, but she figured she would humor him and see where it all went.

"Try me." Her voice shook slightly as she spoke, and she realized the rest of her body was, too.

He smiled, raising his eyebrows. "If I tell you to switch trains at the next station and go home, you will not listen. I know this, and everything else that is going to happen once you exit this train."

"Why would I want to do any of that?" Curious, Marley was leaning in, listening carefully now, and waiting for some of what he was saying to gel in her mind.

"A series of unfortunate events will occur today. They're all leading up to a fateful moment which I cannot fully reveal to you." The stranger rubbed his hands together. "Knowing the future often prompts people to change their natural reactions, thus altering the course of time." He sat up taller and got closer to Marley.

"What are you, psychic or something? Is that what all of this is?"

He shrugged. "Something." The stranger looked at the car as if to make sure no one was there to hear what he was about to say. "I'll keep it simple for you, Marley. But you must pay attention to every single word I say so as each event occurs, you will have the confirmation you need to know that I am telling the truth."

"Go on." Marley held her breath as she waited for his next words.

"Your train arrives at your destination around 3:47 pm. It will be three minutes late according to the printed schedule. Once you're there, you will receive a message from Jennifer, your sister, telling you that she is running late. Then, she'll ask to meet you at Joe's Cafe a half hour later than you expected." He took a deep breath. "However, Jennifer will not meet you at Joe's Cafe. Instead, you will run into her roommate, Amy, there. She will offer to take you to her apartment."

Marley parted her lips to ask a question, but quickly closed them when it evaporated on her tongue.

The stranger pursed his lips. "Here's where the trouble begins, so listen carefully, Marley." He paused and seemed to gather himself for the rest of the discussion. "Amy knows Jennifer is not coming to meet you. Amy is certain of this because she knows exactly where Jennifer is, and given her situation, she is unable to meet you." He folded his hands as if to pray. "I will tell you now that you should not go with Amy because it's not safe by any means. In fact, it's terribly dangerous."

Marley felt gooseflesh forming and couldn't help herself from asking. "Dangerous? How so?"

The stranger leaned in much closer to Marley and then lowered his voice to a whisper. "Even if you had never met me on this train, but especially because you did, you will end up going along with Amy. And because of your decision, your life will also be in danger."

Marley's shiver had evolved into a shake and she found herself gaping at the old man's words. "That's insane."

He paused for a few moments, looking deep into her eyes. "I can't tell you anything more than I already have, but I will give you an escape hatch, of sorts." The man opened his dusty suit jacket and pulled out a faded business card from the inner pocket. Looking it over a moment, he massaged it between his fingers before handing it to Marley. "This place will save you," he said.

Marley examined the card. She noticed there was no name and no phone number on the card, only an address. "What is this, a joke?"

The man raised his eyebrows. "No, it's not a joke at all. It's the only place in the world you will ever be out of harm's way." The stranger looked down at Marley as he rose. "Now that I've said my peace, it's time for me to be on my way." He reached down, grabbed her hand and gave it a squeeze. "Remember all that I have told you. And most of all, avoid the imminent danger that lies ahead."

As he turned to leave, Marley stretched her arm out to reach for him one last time, but he slipped from her grasp. She stood to ask the question that had been burning a hole in her mind since the stranger arrived—who are you? As the words she had been yearning to speak fell out of her mouth, she realized he had seemingly vanished into thin air.

{THREE}

FAITHFUL TO THE stranger's word, Marley's train pulled into her destination's station precisely three minutes later than the time the transportation pamphlet originally promised. While it could have been coincidental or lucky guesswork, Marley was curious about how the rest of the old man's guessing game would pan out.

She checked her phone the moment she stepped onto the railroad platform. Sure enough, she had missed a text from Jenn during her trip. Service on the train was spotty at best, and she had been reading.

Studying the text, her sister didn't mention Joe's Cafe, as the stranger predicted she would. Instead, Jenn's message confirmed the meeting place they both had decided upon last night. It was the coffee shop in the station house.

Marley breathed a sigh of relief. Of course, it all made sense now. That silly old man told her a story, an outrageous tale. He probably saw her sitting there all alone on the train reading a book and thought that she could use some drama and adventure in her real life. She laughed aloud at no one, relieved at what had turned out to be an outrageous story.

She felt lighter, as though she were floating, as she pressed on toward the coffee shop to meet her sister.

Although she was certain the stranger's remaining predictions were bogus, she refused to toss away the business card he had given her. Even if it was far-fetched and unbelievable, she wasn't willing to roll the dice on safety in any situation.

Halfway over to meet Jenn, Marley's phone vibrated. She looked down at the screen and saw it was another text message from her sister.

"I need a few more minutes. I'm sorry. Can you meet me at Joe's Cafe instead? Of course, you can! I'll see you in a half hour. XO."

Marley pulled up short. Could the old man on the train have been right after all? If so, she was seeing the future come to life and it terrified her. What would happen next? She had no idea and didn't want to take any chances.

She pressed 9 and then 1 on her phone, then stopped. Realizing she had nothing of value to say to the cops that wouldn't sound completely made up or insane, she did what her sister expected. She shut off the phone. She made her way to the street and hailed a cab to Joe's café instead.

Once there, Marley tried to relax a little. She ordered a latte and sat down at an empty table by the front window in the shop to wait for Jenn.

A tinny voice coming from across the coffee shop, one not belonging to Jenn. It caught Marley's attention. "Marley? Is that you?"

She looked up to see a blonde girl coming over to her table. "I'm sorry, do I know you?"

The girl pulled a chair out from the other side of the table and took a seat. "Oh my gosh, I'm so rude. Hi, I'm Amy. I'm Jenn's roommate. I recognized you from all of the photos Jenn has around."

Immediately, her palms grew sweaty. It was all happening and exactly the way the stranger had said it would.

Marley swallowed hard, putting on her best fake smile. She reached her hand out to Amy. "Hey, great to meet you."

When Marley took Amy's hand, her palm was cold and clammy. "Sorry to freak you out. I knew you were meeting Jenn, of course. I figured I would surprise you guys and meet you, too." Amy's voice carried a hint of knowing that Marley didn't like.

Marley began looking around, wondering why her sister was so late. Too much time had passed and it didn't make sense. It wasn't like Jenn to be late, let alone twice in one day unless something was wrong.

She checked her phone again, and still there were no new messages that had come through. "Where's Jenn?"

A sinister look flickered across Amy's face, but she quickly recovered with a smile. "Oh, you know how she is, such a workhorse. She's probably still at the office." Her smile switched a millisecond too quickly to a frown.

Tiny hairs all over Marley stood on end. "True. I'll just give her a call and let her know I'm waiting here with you." She began her brave acting again with a smile. "She'll be happy to know we're together." She picked up her phone to dial her sister when she felt Amy's hand on top of hers, pushing it down onto the table.

"Don't bother," Amy said. "You know she won't answer when she's working on a project." She stood and tapped Marley as if to say she should get up too. "If she's not here yet, she's probably not coming. I think it's a good idea if we head back to our place. I can take you there now." Amy picked up her cell phone and looked like she was typing something. "I'm just going to let her know we'll be back at the apartment soon so she can meet us there."

Marley was beyond suspicious and her body responded. The bees buzzing in her gut wouldn't let up. Something terrible was going to happen and she should go to the police now, and then go to Jenn's apartment with an escort. The stranger had told her not to go with Amy. But he had also told Marley she would go anyway.

Marley twirled her hair around her finger in contemplation. She glanced back down at her phone, but there were no new text messages from Jenn saying she was going to be late. Her heart began to pound and she wondered if Amy could hear the fear escaping her chest. There were no choices for Marley to make any longer, nothing at all to consider. No matter the consequences, she had to take action and fast.

Marley tossed her cell phone back into her purse and stood up. "Sounds good. Let's get going." Then she followed Amy into a nearby cab, unable to speak and unable to breathe but determined to find out the truth.

{FOUR}

JENN AND AMY'S apartment door was ajar, which didn't seem right to Marley. "Do you always leave your front door wide open?"

"No, not usually." Amy's head shot left to right as if she were looking for someone in the hallway. "Jenn probably came home in a rush and didn't close it all the way." She seemed concerned, pausing slightly before pushing the front door fully open and walking inside her apartment. "We're home! Marley's with me. Where are you at, girl?"

Marley entered the main room cautiously, both expecting to see her sister and also remembering what the stranger told her on the train.

Your life will be in danger.

"That's odd," Amy said as she looked around. "Jenn should definitely be home by now, but she's not here." She turned to face the hallway. "I'll be right back. I'm going to check the bedrooms. Make yourself at home, okay?"

19

"Okay." Marley found a seat on the couch, uncomfortable but unsure of what to do next. She knew Jenn wasn't home yet because her sister would have met her at the door, or responded to their calls aloud at the very least. Marley checked her phone to find no new messages from Jenn, which didn't make sense. She definitely would have said she was running even later than she had expected.

After several minutes passed with no response, Marley couldn't wait any longer. She was starting to get concerned about Jenn's whereabouts and knew instinctively that something was definitely wrong. Marley didn't just send her sister another text message, she called her cell phone.

That's when she heard it...Jenn's cell phone was ringing nearby. In fact, the sound was coming from the kitchen. Marley couldn't understand how her sister could have left her cell phone at home, the same one she had been using to text with all day. None of it made any sense.

No matter, Marley followed the ringtone all the way into the kitchen, where she took a good look around. But what she found wasn't Jenn's cell phone. Instead, she spotted her sister's red tennis shoe. It was protruding from the corner of the kitchen that met the oversized pantry.

Marley's stomach dropped. She took a few steps closer and her darkest fears were confirmed. It was Jenn's sneaker all right, but it wasn't supposed to be red—it was meant to be a white sneaker, except now it was drenched in blood.

Jenn's crimson body lie sprawled in the center of the ceramic tiles, her long, brown curls had gelled together from being soaked in congealed fluids. Her formerly crystal blue eyes were wide open, a horror beyond anything Marley had ever seen. Now, they were covered in a cloudy film, dulled in their death. Valleys in Jenn's open flesh overflowed with a thick pudding-like substance, exposing her insides.

Marley covered her mouth quickly, afraid she was going to vomit at any moment. The dead body on the floor looked nothing like her sister, yet her heart knew it was Jenn.

The horror right before Marley's eyes, both of the murder and loss of her sister, was unbearable. She wailed and it was unrecognizable to her. Someone else had undoubtedly been screaming, somebody else's sister was the girl who was dead.

Amy stepped into the kitchen, only to back out slowly, blindly grabbing for the cordless phone on the wall. "Oh my God! What is this, Marley?"

"Call the police!" Marley was still in hysterics and relying on Amy to be the responsible one in the most horrifying situation she had ever endured. All Marley could bring herself to do was to collapse on the floor at her sister's feet and cry. "No. Please, God, no."

A few moments later, the front door flew open. Marley prepared herself mentally to confront the police and relay the events of the day, including the old stranger on the train. She wiped her tears with the back of her hand, took a deep breath and stood to confront the officers.

Instead of seeing the cops, she practically ran right into a man in the doorway. He looked oddly familiar, although Marley was convinced she had never seen him before.

The man ignored her and hugged Amy instead. "Everything is going to be okay."

Marley shook her head, confused. She examined his familiar features. She had seen him before, she was certain. Examining the mantel, her heart raced. Sure enough, he was the same guy locked in a loving embrace with her sister, Jenn in the photo on the ledge. Turning back toward them, Marley saw the man put his hand Amy's lower back and smile.

"What's going on here?" Marley asked in a panic. "Where are the police?"

Amy shot Marley a look of power. "They're on their way so stay put."

That's when the man took a step toward Marley. "This is all your fault, you know. And you're going to prison for a very, very long time."

They both started laughing, but Marley was horrified. "You're both crazy. Insane!" They were going to frame her for her own sister's murder. Marley had no choice but to flee the apartment right away.

When she took a step, both of them tried to block the doorway, but Marley was too fast. In the breath before they grabbed her, she squeezed between them and ran out the door.

Marley took off sprinting down the stairway as fast as her feet could take her. She kept on running until she was out of breath entirely. Finally, what had to have been a mile away from her sister's crime scene, she fell hard on the grimy, city sidewalk.

There, Marley frantically searched her purse until she found the stranger's business card. She held it between her fingers for what seemed like forever, before deciding what to do next. Then, she picked herself up, brushed herself off and hailed an empty taxi cab to the address listed.

Whatever was in store for her, even if it put her life in danger, she resolved to see her story through to the bitter end.

{FIVE}

"**H**ONEY CAN YOU hear me? The soft hand on her arm, coupled with the light, airy voice in the distance told Marley her mother was speaking to her. To be sure, Marley looked around with intent to confirm her suspicions, but she couldn't see much of anything. The stark white walls blinded her, reflecting the fluorescent lighting from above. She squinted her eyes until they were able to focus a bit. Her senses were on high alert. The scent of alcohol burned her nostrils and made her eyes tear. The desert-quality air turned the inside of her mouth into sandpaper. It was unpleasant at best.

Through foggy vision, Marley vaguely made out the silhouette of her mother. "Mom, what's going on? Where am I?"

Her mother kissed her lightly on the forehead. "Oh, dear. Here we go again."

Out of nowhere, the stranger from the train appeared. Instead of his all black ensemble, he was

25

wearing all white now. "I can see that you are upset. Please try to calm down."

Marley tried to get her mental bearings, but it wasn't nearly impossible. She didn't understand why the old man was in the room with her and more mother. More urgently, she had to tell her mother about what happened to Jenn.

Emotions came to her like a flood and she began sobbing. In between bursts of tears, she explained. "Mom, I found Jenn. She's dead. Someone murdered her and I think it was her roommate, Amy. We need to call the police."

Marley's mother came into view again, with the stranger stepping back. "Hush now. It's okay, honey. Just take a deep breath and try to relax."

"No, you don't understand. She's dead. Your daughter was killed. Why aren't you calling the police?" Marley was borderline hysterical, but she couldn't understand why no one was reacting to the news that Jenn had been murdered.

Marley's disorientation escalated further when she spotted Jenn standing next to her mother. "Oh my, God. Jenn, you're alive!"

Marley's sister held her hand as she spoke. "Honey, I'm not Jenn. I'm Amy, your other sister."

"I don't understand." Marley shook her head, trying to clear it. She was mixing things up, that was all. She attempted to lift herself so she could sit upright, but the pressure bearing down on her was more than she could handle. When she glanced down, she saw the reason for her obstacle. Thick white straps ripped into her arms and pressed down on her chest. She was tied down for some reason, one she couldn't understand except that maybe seeing Jenn's murder had pushed her over the edge, although she couldn't recall hysterics. She would have to fight her way up, so she attempted to kick wildly. That's when she realized her legs were immobile from the metal braces imprisoning her ankles and thighs. "What have you done to me?"

The stranger from the train was back, leaning over her now. "Confronting the tragic event was certain to initiate a post-traumatic flashback."

Marley's eyes darted around, looking for a savior. "Let me go. You can't restrain me like this. Mom? Amy? Please help me." From Marley's peripheral vision, she spotted her mother and sister locked in a sorrowful embrace, not moving in response to her pleas.

The old man continued. "It's important for you to realize the truth. You didn't find your sister, Jenn, murdered."

"You're wrong. I was there. I saw her body with my own eyes. I smelled her blood. I . . ." The memory of her sister's body flooded her mind and heart, and she lost all sense of control again.

"Five years ago this week, you took a train into the city." The stranger paused. "Marley, this is going to be difficult to hear, but it must be said if you are ever to recover."

"You're wrong." Marley couldn't believe the lies they were telling her. There were so many lies.

"You walked in on Jennifer and your fiancé. Marley, your sister, betrayed you. Jennifer was dating your fiancé, the same man you were engaged to marry. The man you loved was cheating on you, with your own sister."

Marley felt her heart pump out of control. He was lying, this old, strange man from the train. She didn't know why, but he was a cold-hearted, crazy liar. "Stop telling me these lies. Dirty, dirty lies."

"You were so upset, Marley, so outraged. You had just been betrayed by your sister and the love of your life."

"That's not true. Jenn would never do that to me. Brad would never do that to me." With the sound of his name on her lips, rage began to bubble up inside of her and she couldn't recall whatever happened to Brad.

"You went into the kitchen and you grabbed a cleaver."

"No, I didn't!"

"Listen carefully, Marley. You took the cleaver and you repeatedly stabbed Jennifer."

"What? You're crazy. I would never stab anyone, especially not Jenn."

"Marley, you did stab her, many, many times, until she died."

Marley snapped her head back and forth savagely, her hair whipping her face. "No. You lie! You're a liar! A dirty, dirty liar!"

"You must know the murder wasn't your fault. Marley, you're a very sick girl. You must realize that first and foremost. You had no control over yourself at that moment."

"Bastard! Why are you doing this to me? Why are you telling me these awful, dirty lies?" Marley slammed her body against the mattress in a vicious rage to both free and harm herself.

"You live here now so you can get help. You are out of harm's way. You're no longer a danger to yourself or to anyone else. You are finally safe." The stranger smiled softly.

"No. You're wrong." Marley's eyes darted upward and she caught a glimpse of fluid spurting out of a large needle. The stranger was pointing the razor tip at her and slowly approaching her upper arm.

Finally, Marley got the answer to her question on the train when she read the stranger's name tag: *Dr. Joseph Stockton, Psychiatrist.*

Images flashed through her mind at super speed. Taking the train home to surprise her fiancé, Brad. His apartment door cracked open. Calling his name with no response. Making her way into his bedroom. The clothes were strewn about. Brad and Jenn locked in a lover's embrace. Brad taking a shower.

The kitchen cleaver. The surprise attack. The tennis shoe. The blood.

The murder.

Marley realized he was telling the truth, and then she began to scream.

THE END

TRAIN GIRL

AGAIN

A Short Story

{ONE}

*L*UCY PRACTICED HER venomous script, role-playing with the vacant chair opposite her. "Today . . . is your last day. Today is your last . . . day. Today is . . . your last day."

As the human resources director, Lucy Matheson wore a plethora of hats at work, many of which she would have preferred to toss. Especially the dark one, the hat that required she fire people with professionalism and grace. She rolled her eyes at the thought. There was no such thing as gracefully firing someone. No matter how one lost their job, it was never pretty.

Lucy straightened, cleared her throat, and then suited her energy up for the person without emotions. She sharpened her tone and demeanor until the message sounded clear, concise, and indisputably final. "Today is your last day." She smiled to herself, pleased with her ability to pull it off.

Tightening the silk scarf around her neck, Lucy recalled the recent meeting with her boss, who also happened to be the CEO and namesake of the firm.

"As you know, once Edmon Enterprises acquired this company, our first order of business was to clean house." Mr. Edmon adjusted his tie as he spoke. "The first week we took over, we promptly walked most of the employees, one by one, straight out the front door. That day wasn't one of my proudest moments, but it was essential to the future of our business. It wasn't personal. It's still hard to believe our mass layoff was six months ago already. Many times it feels like yesterday." He closed his eyes and shook his head at the memory.

Lucy remained silent since there was no easy way to agree or disagree with him. She had heard all about the terrible day in the company's history and was very grateful she had not been around at that point.

"As I'm certain you've heard, management wasn't prepared to handle the mayhem that ensued from the remaining staff after that massacre. No one was productive for weeks. They spent their days crying, or gossiping, or calling out sick in protest. Rumors started spreading like wildfire around here. The employees left behind were in an uproar. And I suppose I can't blame them one bit."

Lucy chimed in, offering her support. "You did the right thing. I know that's not always popular with everyone, but it is business, not personal like you said."

He pursed his lips. "Well, that may be true, but look at it from their point of view. Hard-working folks were forced to sit back and watch helplessly as their coworkers, their friends, carried cardboard boxes filled with years' worth of belongings out to their cars."

"It must have been a difficult time." Lucy gave him her best sympathetic look. She had been hired shortly after that incident, essentially walking into the aftermath of a war zone. It hadn't been an easy transition for anyone to have a new hire show up amongst a sea of terminations.

Mr. Edmon continued. "Your accomplishments in the Human Resources industry are very impressive. Did you know your nickname behind closed doors is *The Terminator*?"

Lucy nodded and felt her face warm. She was compelled to explain her often-misguided nickname. "It's not something I brag about, but yes, it's a part of my job that I take quite seriously." An apologetic half-smile was all she could muster.

"And you're damned good at it, Ms. Matheson." Mr. Edmon's expression lit up, as though he were proud of her. Then it quickly turned serious.

"That's why you're the one who's going to handle Edmon Enterprise's final termination."

Lucy scrunched her face in confusion. "I'm sorry if I misunderstood, but I thought we eliminated all of the positions from Volger Industries already?"

"That's mostly true." Mr. Edmon shrugged. "However, given the sensitive circumstances when a corporate firm acquires a family business, we made an exception for one employee."

Tatiana. The name came to Lucy like a tsunami. How had she forgotten? A sharp pain electrified her chest, and she put a hand over her heart. The twinge of an impending panic attack always rocked her world, even more so after her parents' unexpected death one year ago. She took a deep breath in recovery and tried to clear her mind, but the reality of her assignment didn't sit well with her.

Tatiana Volger, the daughter of the firm's founder and lone survivor of Volger Industries, was still employed. And she was untouchable.

Despite the distaste of the undertaking, Mr. Edmon was giving Lucy an opportunity to prove herself. Decidedly, she was ready to step up to the plate and swing.

{TWO}

LUCY MATHESON SHUDDERED as her office door flung open unexpectedly, and Tatiana Volger sauntered in.

After arranging her body into a composed form, Lucy clasped her hands together to mask her nerves. "Ms. Volger, please have a seat."

The woman's raven locks were a severe contrast to the pale eyes that seemed to be protruding from her skull. Straight out of a horror movie, a frosty breeze trailed the ice-eyed lady, blowing strands of hair past her wrinkled brow. The gossip and whispers that Lucy had heard about Tatiana now birthed goose bumps on Lucy's arms.

Tatiana practiced the devil's work, people said. She had powers . . . Maybe she was even a witch. No matter what was true or false, people stayed away from her, and for good reason. She was terrifying to look at, even more so if the rumors were partially true. Lucy had experienced enough darkness in her life. She certainly didn't need any more black clouds following her around.

Regardless of her unsettled feeling, Lucy was a professional. She stuck firmly to her script and carried on with the task at hand. "Despite efforts to streamline costs, the company is still over budget on staffing expenses." Lucy paused for a moment before continuing. "Effective immediately, your position has been eliminated." She swallowed hard and then took a deep breath before she spoke the words all employees feared. "Today is your last day."

Be the decision wrong or right, be the whispers true or false, Lucy was following orders. The choice wasn't hers, but the realization gave her the confidence she needed to finish the meeting.

Tatiana's vision seared into the human resources director, although, the raven-haired woman never uttered a sound.

Lucy continued. "We are offering you a severance package to help with this difficult transition." She felt Tatiana's stare grow deeper and denser with each word spoken, like a knife boring slowly into her chest. "Once you sign the Agreement," Lucy said, pausing to slide an envelope across the desk. "There is a seven-day waiting period before we can issue you the lump sum severance payment."

Tatiana remained silent, yet she continued to scrutinize Lucy, her eyes narrowing until they were slits.

Finding herself intimidated by the woman yet again, Lucy took a deep breath to calm herself before finishing. "However, a silver lining is that you can continue your benefits for up to eighteen months under the law, for which Edmon Enterprises will pay one-hundred percent."

On and on, Lucy went. And on and on, Tatiana glared.

When the meeting adjourned, Tatiana did not move. She remained as still as stone.

True to her training, Lucy methodically moved the tissue box from her side of the desk to within Tatiana's reach, expecting the usual tears once the shock of the job loss had dissipated.

Instead of tears, Tatiana's bony arm launched from her lap. Her gnarled hand clutched Lucy's wrist hard. She winced but had no time to react because it all happened so fast. With the other hand, Tatiana fondled the bronze medal draped around her neck. Her crystal irises vanished as she swayed, mumbling an undecipherable verse with closed eyes. Then, in one fluid motion, the horrifying scene was over as fiercely as it began. Tatiana was motionless, her eyes transfixed on the space beyond Lucy.

Lucy considered reacting but was in too much shock to do anything.

Without warning, Tatiana released her rooting from the chair and headed for the door. Just before exiting, she pivoted slightly and caught Lucy's gaze one last time.

Then she whispered one, terrifying word. "Again."

{THREE}

O N THE DRIVE LIPS home from work, Lucy couldn't help but feel uneasy. It was as if someone was watching her every move, yet she knew she was alone.

At the stoplight before turning down her street, she decided to ease her mind and confirm her assumption. Lucy checked the rearview mirror and then turned around to make sure she hadn't missed anyone hiding in her backseat.

Without relief and still feeling as though she had an invisible companion nearby, she turned up the radio instead. Lucy wanted nothing more than to take her mind off of the day that didn't make sense, but the foreboding seemed to be growing in intensity the closer she got to home.

Typically a pro at leaving her work stress at work, Lucy brought it, or something, home with her today. And it was something she couldn't shake off no matter how hard she tried.

As Lucy pulled into her driveway, the chills that had been forming intensified. She took a deep breath and opened the car door. Heading toward her house, she spotted an odd sight. It was a crow, not a familiar creature to appear in her neighborhood. In fact, she couldn't recall a time she had ever seen one, except perhaps in a horror movie.

Lucy stared up at the tree, examining the bird for a few moments. It seemed to consider her right back as it sat silently perched upon a rotting limb above her head. Then its ebony wings fluttered, shimmering in the dusky fog. The jet-black bird moved its head slightly to peer past the decomposing branches.

It was acknowledging her appearance.

Lucy took a few steps back. She hugged herself, shivering, as she stood there, unable to move while exchanging silent glances with the dark creature.

Once inside, Lucy tried to shake off her thoughts of her odd encounter with the creepy bird and began her nightly routine of feeding her cat, Whiskers, instead. Once he was eating, she emptied what was left in the bottle of Bordeaux on her counter into a stemless wine glass.

No matter how she tried to distract herself, her workday had left her inexplicably shaken. She had done exactly what her boss had expected of her, and she had done it well. It did not stop the negativity from breeding in her soul and spreading with deadly intent. Impending doom was all Lucy felt, and she couldn't help but think it had something to do with Tatiana's strange behavior in the office.

Lucy slumped on the couch with her wine to sift through the mail. One of the pieces was a large bundle from Arnold J. Stevens, Esq., which grabbed her attention. She was far from a person who got into trouble, so what would an attorney want from her? It couldn't be anything good.

With her stomach fluttering in anticipation of some terrible news, she ripped the envelope seal open with her nail. Just as Lucy suspected, the enclosed document named her, Ms. Lucinda Matheson, as the defendant in a lawsuit from a car accident almost two years ago—narrowly within the statute of limitations. She had already forgotten about it, yet it had come back to haunt her with a vengeance.

The paperwork stated that Dr. Francine Watkins had been deemed "permanently disabled" as a result of Ms. Matheson's negligent driving. Dr. Watkins was seeking compensation for "lost wages" in conjunction with the accident. Lucy's quick math revealed that after her insurance company paid the claim, her personal liability for crashing into the accomplished surgeon's SUV, not counting the unknown amount of medical bills, would be six to seven figures—more than she had ever seen, or ever would see, in her back account.

Lucy needed an attorney of her own, and a boatload of good luck, neither of which she imagined would be easy to obtain.

She tossed the paperwork on the coffee table, chugged the entire glass of wine, and went upstairs.

Retreating to her bedroom in angst, Lucy went through the rest of her evening ritual hoping it would put her in a better state of mind. She removed her watch and silver hoops and placed them in her jewelry box. While it was open, something told her to take note of the contents. Sure enough, her gut instinct was on point. Her mother's two-and-a-half-karat diamond ring was missing. It was always there, like a lighthouse on her darkest days. She never wore it, but seeing it there gave her comfort.

Where could it have gone? Her heart began to beat out of her chest. *Had she been robbed?*

Lucy sifted through her jewelry box in a frantic frenzy, inspecting every worthless piece of metal only to come up empty-handed. It was as though the ring had disappeared. There had to be an explanation. Maybe it had been tangled up in another piece of jewelry and had gotten misplaced in one of her rushes out the door in the morning. She was always five minutes off and trying to play catch up. That had to be it. No matter, Lucy was going to find her mother's ring. It meant too much to her. It meant everything.

Lucy closed the jewelry box and moved on to her bedroom at large. She spent the next half hour ripping it apart from top to bottom. Nothing was off limits. She even crawled underneath the bed to search like a bloodhound for the vanished rock. She probed below the dressers, moving dust bunnies as she eyeballed the floor and everything on it. In her closet, every shred of clothing was taken off the hanger and twisted inside out, examining every single garment.

With no luck, Lucy fell heavily onto her down comforter. Her room looked like a tornado had hit it, yet she still hadn't been able to find the single remaining relic of her mother. The ring had also dearly departed.

Her heart, already utterly broken by loss, ached. She had lost the one thing that connected her to her mother on a physical level. It was almost too much for her to bear.

Lucy scanned her bedroom for her inhaler. On top of the paralyzing anxiety, she had developed asthma. She often forgot how much the two were connected, one regularly causing the other to rear its ugly head. She had gotten herself so upset; she hadn't even realized what was happening.

Of course, she couldn't find the damn thing when she needed it most. And now her panic was setting in, silently coaxing her airways to constrict even faster until she passed out. Lucy tried to calm herself and wheezed deeply to recover her breath, but it wasn't working. Anxiety and asthma were working together against her. On a scale of one to ten, her dual attacks were rapidly increasing to an eight.

Refusing to lose complete control, Lucy attempted to keep her mind clear as she hunted down her nebulizer. Once she was able to focus, she spotted the medical device on the far corner of her dresser. She seized it, then began puffing with intensity until she lassoed the medication into her lungs, and could breathe again.

Exhausted, Lucy gave up on her ring hunting for the moment and decided that spending the night on the couch with Whiskers was in order. And, more importantly, another bottle of wine.

Right before she reached the stairs, she could have sworn a single black feather billowed onto the carpet in her peripheral vision. But when she turned around to see if she was hallucinating, it was gone.

{FOUR}

INSTEAD OF SUFFOCATION Lucy resolved herself to drowning in her favorite red wine. Oak and cherries permeated her taste buds as she swigged a desperate mouthful. Her muscles relaxed on cue. Nothing pleased her quite like the flavor of a fantastic fermented grape on her tongue. It was sheer perfection.

Lifting the kitchen window, she leaned out to suck in the crisp night air. She took a vigorous, chest-heaving breath, which combined with the wine, instantly calmed her. She felt like herself again, normal and at peace. The day had been a calamity of terrors, and she was ready to put it all to rest. Too often, she allowed outside influences to affect her inner serenity. It was something she needed to get control over if she was ever going to rise above the horrors she had experienced in her life.

Becoming an orphan could have been the worst thing ever to happen to her if she let it. She was determined to live, in honor of her parents, since they didn't have that luxury. And no one, not even Tatiana Volger, was going to influence her into living in fear of what was to come. Lucy had already experienced the worse thing in life, to lose one's parents at such a young age. There was nothing that anyone could do to hurt her more than that. The worst part of her life was over.

She took one last breath and smiled. As she withdrew inside the window, the crow appeared once again. This time, it was apparently fixated on her with its neck stretched out, head tilted in an apparent effort to understand her. Its eyes grabbed hers and held on tight.

Lucy shuddered. It couldn't be what she thought—a dark bird, an omen of some kind passed down from a disturbed and jaded woman. The lawsuit, the missing ring—they were all a coincidence. It was all an unexplainable plot dreamed up by Lucy's paranoid head.

Still, she felt the need to test the creature and her sanity. Standing tall and firm, Lucy slid slightly to the left center of the window. The crow's gaze followed her, its head changing course until aligned with hers. Then, Lucy shifted to the right and waited. Soon after, the crow's body mimicked her movement exactly. It was uncanny and terrifying. Finally, she swiveled around and then backed towards the window. The crow mirrored her actions, every twist, and turn. When done with the odd dance, it remained concentrated on her next move.

But there wouldn't be one. Lucy knew better than to test darkness, which is what the crow was to her—all that was evil and dark in this world. And she knew in the deepest bowels of her soul, Tatiana had done something to send the crow to her.

Lucy's body trembled, and her heart slammed against her chest as if it were the ground beneath a herd of horses.

Lucy knew instinctively and without question that the evil bird was tracking her every movement.

A crash shook the second floor of Lucy's house, and she jumped. There were no storms in the area, no lightning, no thunder. She had no idea what it could have been, but she had to find out.

The only logical explanation in her mind was an intruder. The one who had taken her mother's ring?

Lucy squared her shoulders. She didn't own any official weapons because guns terrified her. So she grabbed a meat cleaver for protection, even if only in her mind, not that she had any idea what she was going to do with it.

Just as she arrived at the bottom of the stairs, she saw an object flying through the air, glinting off of the foyer light and then landing at her feet. She bent down to see what it was—her mother's diamond. Lucy quickly retrieved it, putting it on her middle finger, the only place it would fit. She kissed it, silently asking her parents to watch over her, and then headed upstairs to find out what in the world was going on.

As Lucy slowly ascended the old staircase, she wielded the large knife in her hand. It was an attempt to convince herself she was prepared to confront whoever broke into her house. About halfway to the top landing, she thought she probably should have called the police instead of trying to act like a heroine in one of her fiction novels. Real life seldom worked out well in her current situations.

Right before she changed her mind, doubling back to grab her phone, a deafening shrill sound echoed around her, practically perforating her eardrums. She instinctively cowered, lifting both of her hands to cover her ears. In doing so, she dropped her only weapon.

When the noise tapered off, she looked to where the painful sound originated. That's when she caught sight of the crow, its glare unwavering. Lucy knew for certain the evil in its gaze was meant for her and her alone.

Staring it down now, she could see its eyes so clearly. They were the color of ice, a familiar and haunting vision that began to make sense.

But before she could react, the crow took off after her, fast and furious. Weightless, its wings unfurled in grand fashion as it propelled off of the top of the landing and crossed the open stairwell.

Once the crow was inside her house, it appeared to be growing until it was much larger than a normal crow. Lucy blinked several times. She was certain she was hallucinating. Maybe she had too much wine? Though unbelievable, her gut instinct told her that the vision before her eyes was as real as anything.

In fact, it looked as though the crow was becoming human sized. Lucy couldn't believe her eyes. She had no idea what to make of it all, but she was frozen in fear, unable to move. Even worse, with every inch closer to her, the bird began to morph into a sight that both shocked and horrified her.

Without warning, powerful bony hands came out of the darkness. They pressed against her chest, pushing her with a tremendous force. Lucy tried to scream for help, but she never got the chance to say a single word.

It all happened so fast and before she knew it, she had lost her footing. She began careening backward, flying through the air. The nape of her neck smashed onto the wrought iron banister first. As if she were in a wrestling ring, she felt strong arms throw her up into the air until she was fully airborne. She was disoriented as she tumbled in what seemed like slow motion.

When she was finally able to open her jaw to howl, her right cheekbone exploded on impact with the wall. Several of her teeth skyrocketed across the room as she writhed in pain. Blood spurted violently in all directions as she flipped and flopped in midair, all the while plunging downward.

In the midst of her body toss, she caught sight of a shadowy figure, now at the top of the landing. It was the same vision that appeared to her in the crow's place, the metamorphosed bird now coming to life.

Snowy eyes flickered beneath the black hooded cloak and all of her hope evaporated. A long-nailed, crooked finger pointed at Lucy and a jarring screech exclaimed the haunting message she had heard once before.

"Again."

Then the world as Lucy knew it faded straight to black.

{FIVE}

WHEN LUCY AWOKE from her unsettling night's sleep, the sight of her popcorn ceiling calmed her. She was in her own bed, resting. Her nightmare about the pending termination meeting that had left her shaken was just that: a dream. She released a heavy sigh of relief. Of course, her brain had created a terrible scenario to address her worst fears, to prepare her for the most unimaginable of situations so she would excel in the real life one. It gave her a sense of confidence for having had the dream. Now, she would be more prepared than ever to handle the day ahead.

Today would be difficult, of course, but she would come out on top, as she always did.

Lucy peeled away the covers and then swung her legs around until they landed the floor. She stretched her muscles, slowly waking herself up. Her heart was racing in anticipation, or anxiety, she couldn't tell. As much as she hated firing people, it was something she prided herself on doing well and today's termination would be the hardest of her career. She was ready.

In the dark room, she heard Whiskers calling to her from afar. It was odd since he always slept on the bed with her, but maybe she had locked him in the closet and didn't realize it.

Lucy glanced around the room but didn't see her cat. His meow was concerning, a continuous and piercing sound that began increasing in volume. It sounded like Whiskers was hurt or afraid. If either were true, she needed to find him, and soon.

Lucy moved around the room looking frantically for her baby. She couldn't find him anywhere he frequently hid. As she approached her closet, which wasn't entirely closed, the door swung open wide sending her back a few steps. A blurred image darted from the closet and disappeared under her bed.

Finding his reaction bizarre, she approached the bed with care. Certainly her cat wasn't afraid of her, so it must be that he was hurt. Taking him to the vet would be a difficult and unexpected task to coordinate today, but she would figure it out. She couldn't just go into work knowing something was wrong. She would need to take care of it.

Peeking under the bed, Lucy gently called out to Whiskers. But instead of coming to her, the cat hissed wildly as if in attack mode. She leaned down, reaching her arm to grab him. Then he did the same, scratching her. She recoiled, shocked and taken aback. He had never done anything like that before and Lucy didn't know what to make of it.

Lucy was bleeding and decided to give it a rest for now. She needed to get ready for work regardless, and would just need to deal with her cat afterward.

She went into the bathroom and turned on the shower, beginning her usual workday ritual.

{SIX}

THE LOUD NOISE startled Kim straight out of a deep sleep. She jumped, sitting upright and looking around. Then, she shook her husband, as she always did. "Wake up. It's happening again."

Bill groaned and turned over. "I told you, the pipes in this house are ancient. Stop waking me up for this. It's ridiculous." He rolled on his side away from Kim, pulling the covers over his head.

"Pipes don't turn on faucets," Kim said. She shook him again. "Get up, please. I want you to take a look at it."

"I'll get up when my alarm goes off."

Kim twisted the sheets in her hands. "I can't wait another half hour. I need to get ready."

"Then, go. What are you waiting for? The water's already on."

"Don't make fun of me. I'm not going in there until you check it out. I want to ensure it's safe."

"Really, it's water, Kim."

"I heard footsteps. Pipes don't make footsteps."

Bill exhaled. "They aren't footsteps. You're half asleep. Go take a shower and wake me up when you're out."

"Ugh. I knew we shouldn't have bought this place." Kim was petting her cat vigorously and noting that he seemed a bit high strung this morning. "But, you insisted. You said the house was in a decent neighborhood. You told me that it was such a great price, so much house for the money. That may be true, but at what cost, Bill? I can't live like this anymore. It's not natural."

"Are we really doing this now? Again?" Bill turned toward her, fury spreading all over his face. "Every single day since we moved in you pull the same crap with me. I have to go to work and deal with people's bullshit all day long. I don't need this nonsense first thing in the morning. It's enough already, Kim. I'm putting my foot down. You need to get over it. Whatever your issues are, you need to understand that this is an old house. Things are going to happen. Floors will creak and we will have odd pipe issues. What do you want from me? This is the only house I could afford when you said you wanted to move. I told you to wait another year so we could

64

get something nicer, but you didn't want to wait. So, this is what we got. Now, you're unhappy and you're making me pay for it with your endless bitching. If I knew this was going to be our life, I would have taken the damn loan from your father and bought the piece of crap new construction you wanted." He slid back under the covers, making a ruckus to get into a comfortable position.

Kim bristled. She wasn't going to let this argument end without getting her way. She wouldn't give in on something so important. "Well, genius, we got what we paid for, didn't we? Now we have to live with this---this evil for the rest our lives!"

Bill propelled himself out of bed. "Damn it. Fine, you win. Just shut the hell up about it, okay?" He stomped into the bathroom and turned off the water. "There, the shower is off. And the bathroom is clear. There's nothing in there, or in here, or anywhere else in the house." He shook his head. "You want to know the truth? The truth is that I have to live with your evil mind games and your evil cat for the rest of our lives. That's the only evil in this house. That's it." Then, he stormed out of the bedroom, slamming the door behind him.

The moment after he left, the shower turned on full force.

"Bill!" Kim held her cat close. "It's happening again."

{SEVEN}

L UCY MATHESON SHUDDERED as her office door flung open unexpectedly and Tatiana Volger sauntered in.

Lucy's day continued on, the same as every day, as Tatiana's curse forced Lucy to die again and again and again.

THE END

TO PRESERVE, PROTECT AND DEFEND

A Short Story

{ONE}

FIONA'S HEART POUNDED in time with the twinkling sequins on her royal blue gown. The word *royal* swam around her in waves until it settled on an imaginary cloud somewhere up above her head. She twirled in front of the full-length mirror, watching her skirt fly up into the air and back down again. Everything about her shined, from her designer shoes to her polished grin.

Looking away from her reflection, she caught a glimpse of her mother standing directly behind her and nearly jumped. It was as if she had appeared out of nowhere.

"Oh, Fiona." Her mother dabbed the corners of her eyes with a handkerchief. "Look at the beautiful woman you have become." She shimmied closer to Fiona until she caught her gaze in the mirror.

Fiona Rockford was hardly a woman at fifteen and a half. She spoke to her mother's reflection, acknowledging the uniqueness of the moment and adding a dash of sarcasm to her tone. "I'm finally the princess you've always wanted."

Her mother placed her cold hands on Fiona's shoulders and then leaned in to kiss her on the cheek. They were both fixated on their own reflections now, two diamonds glimmering like the colors of the American flag.

"You've always been our princess. Now, you belong to our great nation as well." She squeezed Fiona tight. "You're a princess for all of us."

She couldn't enjoy the moment, she was too annoyed. "Mom, my dress." Fiona wiggled away from the chilly grasp, gooseflesh forming on her arms. Her reaction may have been obnoxious, but tonight was important to her. She was going to be a star on television.

"Oh, dear. What have I done?" Her mother used her palms to smooth the creases in the satin around Fiona's neckline, trying to reverse the damage done. They both knew her dress was to be admired, not touched.

Fiona rolled her eyes. "Honestly, Mother. You're the First Lady. Isn't there someone else who can fix my dress? Surely, you have more important things to do this evening."

Priscilla's eyes were connected with her daughter, Fiona. When those green irises flickered, her mother's pupils contracted slightly. For a moment, it looked as though she were wearing contacts meant to imitate cat eyes. "It's called taking care of my daughter, which falls exactly under the definition of my role as your mother. And, you know that no one can be your mother but me."

Fiona had no right to argue with her mom, especially not on such an important evening for the nation. However, they both knew that someone else, someone Fiona had never met, had also been her mother once.

The First Lady stood back admiring Fiona's appearance, one that had taken several hours, and many people, to create. Her mother drew in a breath. "Perfection. Sheer perfection."

Fiona's grin was speckled with innocence. "You don't look so bad yourself."

No one would argue that she was a spoiled child. She knew nothing other than entitlement in her life, and she wasn't one who ever gave compliments. But, her blatant admiration for her mother tonight was the understatement of the century. Priscilla Rockford was drop-dead gorgeous in the floor-length, crimson silk gown that hugged her tall, slim figure. For a fifty-year-old, she was model worthy, and no different looking than Fiona remembered as a child. There wasn't a wrinkle on her mother's skin, not even a faint line of an impending crow's foot. She had no gray hair either, and as far as Fiona knew, her mother's stylist never touched her with hair dye. It was all natural and breathtaking. Her perfect chestnut waves draped down her back like a Hollywood starlet from the 1950's. She was a natural stunner.

On the contrary, Fiona's milky-white complexion and hay-colored locks destined her to remain an ugly duckling forever. Makeup artists and the like could only go so far. When you had tainted genes, there was little hope. Fiona knew this but pretended otherwise. For once in her life, she wanted to be the one who turned heads, even if only in her mind.

Her mother curtsied before leaving. "Fifteen minutes until showtime."

When she left, Fiona stood alone with the plethora of staff picking and prodding at her in her new White House bedroom. As the family of Reid Rockford, the former Governor of Nevada, she was no stranger to the black-tie events that accompanied a political existence. Still, no one could have prepared her for the extravaganza of a lifetime—The United

States Presidential Inaugural Ball. It was a dream come true for Fiona, and she intended to treasure every single moment she had in the spotlight. Who knew how long it would last?

Fiona huffed. There were always people around her. She needed a few minutes alone to mentally prepare for the new life she was about to embark upon in the upcoming years. When she finally shrugged off the useless staff, they all responded appropriately by scurrying away in silence. A final exhale, and Fiona was ready to take one last look at herself in the mirror. Now when she smiled at herself, she felt it in her heart. She was full of pure excitement.

Tonight, Fiona would be the princess she had always wanted to be. The famously coveted celebrity that every impressionable girl in the nation envied. She wouldn't be surprised if they made little Fiona dolls so young girls would have a respectable idol instead of those mainly naked reality stars. And why shouldn't they make a doll in her likeness? Her father was the President of the United States, after all.

Let the bowing begin, my people. Fiona, your faithful princess, has arrived.

{TWO}

WHEN THE PRESIDENTIAL family arrived at the National Air & Space Museum, Fiona glowed at the fanfare surrounding them. It was more like a blockbuster movie premiere than a traditional government-sponsored event. With the red carpet below her feet and the overabundance of cameras flashing in unison, she was overwhelmed with where to look first.

Nearly blind, Fiona had no idea who lined the path on either side of them, but she reveled in the roar of their cheers nonetheless. Hoots and hollers boomed from every angle. Although likely meant for her father, Fiona smiled as widely as she could, tilted her head up high and rolled her shoulders back. She pretended like the admiration was for her alone. In truth, she was famous now and should act as such.

On her father's arm, the most celebrated man in the country—in the world—Fiona felt like a million dollars wrapped in diamonds. She was indeed guaranteed a date to the prom. Hell, she could demand anyone she wanted to take her, no matter her looks. Finally, she would get the respect she long deserved.

Once inside the extravagant building, an army of secret service officials ushered the presidential family to their honorary seats.

Fiona's agent, Graham Johnson, stuck to her like glue. She huffed. "You're too close. Please back off a bit." She was harsh and rude, but she wanted some freedom in the spotlight.

"It's my job, Miss Fiona. I've been given direct orders not to leave your side," Graham said sternly.

Miss Fiona? She stepped away from him a few inches. "You're ruining my new image. I'm sure you know who's here to see me." The President promised her that Trent Dixson, the lead singer of the hottest band around, would show up. Of course, Trent was there. Her father was the most reliable man on the planet, and he was always true to his word. Her daddy never let her down, and so Fiona always got what she wanted . . . always.

Graham smiled. "I'm quite aware that millions of people will have all eyes on you from here on out, starting with tonight, Miss Fiona."

Her heartbeat skipped at the thought. She temporarily forgot why she was angry in the first place. It felt unbelievably empowering to be the center of everyone's attention. The high only lasted a moment, and then she was back to her usual demanding state of mind.

"Right. Well, Trent Dixson, the lead singer of One Nation is here. I'm sure you've heard of them. The last thing I want is for Trent to be deterred in any way from speaking to me. Do you understand?" She ordered him around with her tone, which was how she had always gotten her way in the past.

With a hand on the weapon at his side, Graham backed up a few feet. "Yes, Miss Fiona, I understand. I will make sure Mr. Dixson gets the proper message from you." He appeared to be giving her enough space to seem alone, but not enough to actually be alone.

Unfortunately, Fiona would just have to learn to live with her shadow, Graham, trailing her for the next four to eight years, at the very least. Her father wasn't going to let go of his throne, as he called it, no matter the rules. Because, as he always said, rules were meant to be twisted apart and ripped to shreds. His philosophy had landed him the presidency, and she intended on following his lead on how to get what she wanted in life, as well. When it worked, it worked.

As the multitude of bands played on, from Grammy winners to timeless legends, Fiona could see how everyone delighted in the music performed in the new president's honor. Truly a joyous occasion was had by all from what she could tell. Fiona especially agreed as she and Trent exchanged flirting glances all night long.

Soon after her parents danced, Fiona took to the stage floor with her father, Mr. President. It was glorious, even more so than she had ever imagined. Her beauty and power were center stage as he lifted her up and swirled her around in front of the entire world. She hung onto him for dear life most of the time, giggles bursting from her so unexpectedly at times that she nearly lost her balance. Fiona snickered with every swoop and dip, feeling more like a six-year-old than an almost-sixteen-year-old. Gratitude didn't come easily for Fiona, yet at that moment, she was beyond grateful that he was her father, the one man who had honest-to-goodness picked her all those years ago. To be chosen was a gift. And she was one lucky, lucky girl.

Fiona whirled along, trying to recall the graceful moves she had learned in her ballroom dancing lessons as they glided across carpets and hardwoods in living rooms all over the globe.

{THREE}

ATER THAT EVENING, the presidential family settled into their new home. In truth, it was hardly settling with the hundreds of staff members rustling around inside the White House. To Fiona's grave disappointment, the exquisite building she had long admired hadn't felt like a home to her at all. It was quite the opposite, actually. The reality of her living there for years to come seemed more like a sentence passed down by a judge, one of isolation and impending doom, maybe even a death penalty. While she hadn't been sure of what to expect going in, carrying the terror of being trapped within massive walls wasn't on her list of anticipated emotions.

Even though it was the White House, it was still going to be her house and it was also meant to be her home. It should have been a place where she felt comfortable, safe and free. A place where she could invite friends for a sleepover, or a movie marathon, or more likely a formal tea party tended to by knowing eyes.

No matter, they were in America where independence reigned, so of course Fiona assumed she would be able to move around freely as she wished. And if not, she would do so anyway. Like her father, Fiona never met a rule she couldn't break with a little coaxing and, when all else failed, sad eyes.

Once all had quieted, from what she could tell, Fiona cracked open her bedroom door, inch by inch, to check out the scene. The house appeared calm and without drama. An uneventful evening was a good evening.

With that, Fiona put one foot out into the hallway. When Graham greeted her seemingly out of nowhere, she jumped slightly.

"Goodness, I didn't see you there." Fiona straightened, trying to act normal.

Graham was all business. "Is there something you need, Miss Fiona?"

She wasn't sure, so she fumbled for an answer. "I . . . I was hoping to get myself a glass of water." What she had said wasn't true, but had made sense. She stood tall, defending her excuse for wandering about the house on her first night there. "I'm thirsty." Without asking permission, Fiona walked completely out of her room. She was about to head to the kitchen when she realized she had no idea where the kitchen was located.

"I can take care of the water for you, Miss Fiona. Do you prefer plain water or sparkling water?"

Sparkling water sounded absolutely delicious to her. She was about to answer Graham but stopped herself. Water wasn't what she wanted. She wanted to explore. "No, that's okay. I'd like to go and get the water for myself." Acting as if it were the most normal thing in the world to do, she asked, "Which way is it to the kitchen?" Fiona squared her shoulders, ensuring he noticed the conviction of her intentions.

"I'll take you there, Miss Fiona. You can come with me." Graham put his arm out to reach for her and guide her along, but Fiona bristled. She straightened her arms at her sides and dug her bare feet into the Oriental rug as if a child disagreeing with her parent. It dawned on her at that moment that not wearing shoes might have been a problem. But since Graham didn't address it, she let it go.

"Thank you, Graham." Fiona realized her forceful attitude wasn't working on him just yet, so she adjusted it. Those things took time and he was new to her style. "It's been a very long day for me." She smiled, forcing innocence in her demeanor from somewhere she had hidden long ago. "Honestly, I would love it if I could take a walk." Fiona paused to emphasize her point. "All by myself." Former presidential families must have been given permission to wander around the house unattended. "Would that be allowable?"

Graham considered her oddly. "Sure, Miss Fiona. Your request can be arranged."

Arranged? She patiently waited for him to alert the staff that she was about to make her way to the kitchen, which is what she assumed he was doing since she couldn't understand a word he was saying. She knew they spoke in code, but hadn't been briefed on the lingo yet, so she was as much in the dark as any enemy of the state.

A few moments later Graham gave her the green light. "All clear, Miss Fiona. You are free to get your glass of water."

He gave her the directions she needed. The route was a series of complex turns in what seemed like a maze. As he spoke, she pretended to be keeping track of it all. Fiona thanked him and then set off to explore the country's largest house of secrets.

{FOUR}

WEAVING IN AND out of a series of nooks and crannies, Fiona passed many White House staffers on the clock for the overnight shift. As she strolled by each one with confidence and purpose, they greeted her with the same salutation as Graham. While she wasn't familiar with the official presidential protocol yet, she knew formalities like 'Miss' had been long dead and buried in her world.

If the staffers knew the truth, they would have stopped her dead in her tracks. Because the truth of it all was that Fiona had absolutely no idea where she was going. Her squared shoulders and steadfast pace screamed intention. However, she was well aware that every person in the White House had been given the green light that she was headed to the kitchen. So, if she wasn't going in the right direction, someone should have gotten in her way and redirected her. Since no one did, Fiona relied upon her feet to lead the way into the unknown.

After about twenty minutes of parading around in what felt like circles, an odd shrieking sound pierced through a nearby blackened hallway. Fiona slowed her pace until stopping at the edge of the opening where the walls met. Cupping her ear, she listened closely.

The noise was unfamiliar and not like anything she had ever experienced, especially not in a home. She couldn't reconcile it with any audible memories, such as a heating vent kicking on or an ice maker regenerating. Then again, it was her first night in the vast and unfamiliar building, one with a history like no other so anything she heard would be new and unidentifiable by her standards.

Still, Fiona was intrigued. She scanned the hallway, and then looked all around for any staffers in sight. No one was there. She was all alone. Ever the arrogant risk taker, Fiona decided to take full advantage of her lone opportunity. After taking a final look around, she darted down the dark alcove like a lightning flash.

To Fiona, it looked more like an alleyway in an impoverished neighborhood than a hallway she would expect to see in the White House. Adrenaline pumped through her as she ran full force toward the high-pitched squeal that sounded like a terrible amateur violinist. For all she knew, the White House had a band that practiced at night. She was in uncharted territory and anything was possible.

The floor dipped low beneath her feet and she found herself running down a ramp that swirled like a broad spiral staircase. The only light left was originating from above her. The lower she went into the darkness, the more frightened she became, but she didn't stop. Fiona might not have had any idea where she was going, but there was no way she was going to turn back now. She had already gone too far down the rabbit hole, and she was so close to getting her answer.

Not only was the unidentified sound louder, but it was clearer. She wasn't far away now. Generally brave, Fiona was uncomfortably terrified with the notion of what she might stumble upon so far down below the earth. Surely only secrets lived here, ones she wasn't privy to, adult or not.

Fiona skidded to a full stop right before she reached the dead end of the hallway. Taking a deep breath, she examined the perplexing sight before her. A seemingly unimpressive door, with a small square window near the top of it, stared her down. A faded glow illuminated the glass, shining the proverbial light at the end of the tunnel her way.

For a brief moment, she considered the notion that she may have had a momentary lapse in her sanity, or perhaps she had died and gone to Hell. Either way, the hair lifting off the back of her neck told her she wasn't in Nevada anymore, and she was pretty sure that wasn't a good thing.

Now that Fiona was practically on top of the sound, she realized the noise she heard earlier wasn't merely one violin, but many playing at different intervals, yet all at once. If she didn't know any better, she would have thought they were musical instruments having a conversation. The tone and inflection of the music replicated words, although it was no language she had ever heard.

Letting her curiosity be her guide, Fiona inched her way to the door. Soon, the only thing left to do was for her to stand on her tiptoes and peek into the illuminated window. With her heart beating out of her chest and her palms soaked in sweat, she took the deepest of breaths. Then on the exhale, Fiona did exactly what she had come there to do, and nothing less than what she had intended.

Fiona looked in the window for the briefest of moments. It must have been long enough because darkness fell upon her and her world faded to black.

{FIVE}

WHEN FIONA FINALLY awoke, it was with a start. The bed was wet, her sheets sweat-soaked through to the mattress. Her pajamas stuck to her like a second skin. She opened her mouth to speak, but it was as dry as the desert where she used to live.

Thankfully, her mother was sitting on her bed, right by her side, holding a glass of water. "Here, honey. Have something to drink."

Fiona must have been making a ruckus in her sleep. Her mother wouldn't have been there waiting for her to wake up if there hadn't been a good reason. No matter, Fiona was too thirsty to question anything. Instead, she grabbed the glass out of her mother's hand and drank it down as fast as possible. The sparkling water Fiona had longed for in her dream refreshed her entirely. When she was done with every last drop, she fell gently into her mother's arms, thankful on multiple levels for the comfort.

The morning light shining through her bedroom window jogged a dark memory. Rushing back all at once was an image of what she had seen when she had peered through the basement window.

Fiona jerked upright, wanting to scream and cry out but she gasped in fright instead. Then wrapped her arms around her mother and squeezed with all of her might.

"Shh, you're safe now, my dear." Fiona's mother held her tight.

"My dream was horrendous. It was the worst kind of nightmare. It was so real, it was as if it all actually happened." Fiona tried to shake off the vision in her mind's eye.

"It's all going to be perfect now." The First Lady stroked Fiona's hair back until it fell away from her face.

She pulled back, wiping her eyes. "I'm sorry that I'm acting like a baby. It's just that my mind was playing tricks on me. I just need a little time to adjust to all of these changes. I promise you, I'll be okay. "

"Of course you will." Her mother got up and walked to the door. "Except sometimes, my dear, your mind isn't the issue after all."

A moment later, the President, Vice President, and the Vice President's wife made their way into Fiona's bedroom. She wasn't expecting company, so she slinked all the way under the covers and then pulled them up to her chin, completely embarrassed. The four most important people in the nation were in her bedroom and she wasn't even dressed yet. Even though two of them were her parents, she was mortified.

"What's going on?" Fiona's voice quivered.

"Darling, there's something you need to know." Her mother glanced at the others, including her father, the President of the United States, as if sending them some kind of signal. They all nodded in unison, responding.

Then, the four of them plodded over to Fiona's bedside like drones being operated by a remote control. She had never seen such a robotic movement in human beings before; to say it was disturbing was an understatement.

Then, one by one, each of the nation's elite reached behind their heads as if performing some synchronized dance, and lifted their skin up off of their heads. Slowly and methodically, they peeled the outer layer of their physical bodies off until it fell completely onto the ground at their feet, then they stepped aside as if it were simply dirty laundry.

What stood before Fiona were four images born out of a horror movie, one she never would have watched. The terror she remembered from her dream the night before wasn't a dream at all. It was her living nightmare and her new reality. Fiona's breath caught in her throat.

Their tiger-striped eyes expanded and contracted as they stared at her, finally revealing their true selves. Their skin, no longer flesh-colored and smooth, was the darkest green and tufted like a reptile's. When they spoke, their voices sounded exactly like the screeching violins she had heard in the White House basement. Only now, she could understand them more clearly than she ever wanted.

"We had no choice, you see," her reptilian father, Mr. President, said. "Humans were killing the planet we needed to inhabit for our future."

Fiona's reptilian mother chimed in. "We never meant any harm, my dear. You must know that you were always part of our master plan. We needed a human child to fit securely into this world. It was the only way humans would ever have accepted us."

Fiona shook her head. "I must be dreaming. Is this really happening? Am I hallucinating, or is this some sick joke? Mom? Dad? Where are you?" She began thrashing her head around, frantically searching for the parents she knew and loved.

The two aliens walked closer to the bed.

"We're right here, dear," her foreign mother said.

"We haven't left you, my darling," her alien father said. "We would never leave you."

Hot tears of fear streamed down her face. "What's going on? Will someone tell me what's happening?"

The third alien, Vice President Zachary Bradly, stepped closer. "We know you're alarmed. It's understandable. Your entire life, actually, the whole world you have lived in has been a lie. But, it's all for the greater good of the universe."

"There's nothing good about this. Where did you monsters take my real parents?" Fiona started to scream, panicking. "Help! Someone, please help me!"

The fourth alien, the Vice President's wife, Camille, spoke next. "There's no one to help you." She rolled her eyes. "So, please stop screaming." She shook her head as if annoyed.

"Calm down, sweetie. There's no reason to get so upset." Her alien mother reached her scaly hand out to touch Fiona.

She slinked away from the reptilian and began crab crawling backward on her wet bed sheets. Her voice was low and thick. "Don't you dare touch me. Get your disgusting skin away from me. You're not my mother. You're not even human. What are you?"

"We're not going to hurt you," her alien father said. "You belong here, with us. That's why we have revealed ourselves to you. We knew we couldn't hide our identities from you forever." The President put his arm around his wife.

"We knew all along you would be the first human to know about us," her alien mother said.

"It was only a matter of time. We just didn't think . . ." The alien Vice President's wife looked to the others. "Well, we didn't think you would find out so soon. The first night? We weren't expecting that."

The four aliens shook as if they were laughing.

"The first human?"

Her strange mother responded. "Oh, you don't remember do you?"

"Remember what?"

"Last night, you found us. All of us."

"All of you?" Fiona was so confused. She was convinced she wasn't awake now. None of what was happening could be real.

"Yes, all of us. Everyone in the White House, the staffers and all. Even Graham, believe it or not. We're all reptilians."

"You can't be serious. You expect me to believe this nonsense?" Fiona studied the ceiling, focusing on the corners where it met the walls. "Where are the cameras? This is some kind of sick joke." She began laughing, partly in terror and partly in insanity.

"It's true, love." The terrifying reptile, President Rockford, made his way to Fiona's bed. "When our planet was destroyed and no longer livable to us, we inhabited the Earth roughly one hundred years ago. It all started on the West Coast where we initially lived in hiding underground, protected by the highest level of military personnel, of course. Not that they had a choice in the matter. Since then, we've been studying humans and today, we're able to blend it quite nicely above ground. In fact, we're practically everywhere in society, with most of us living amongst humans. Although, humans have proven themselves incapable of managing their own race. And, after a long time leaving the earth in their hands, we realized it was time to take control, starting with the oval office."

Fiona twisted in disgust. "Are you saying humans aren't running our country?"

They all shook vigorously, apparently laughing. "Hardly," her father said. "Human beings are the minority on this planet. In fact, they aren't even running the world. We are."

That's when it came back her. She didn't just see one creature through the glass, as she initially recalled, but hundreds of reptiles all gathered in the secret room underground.

"Oh my, God." Fiona began to shake uncontrollably.

"Now that we have secured the presidency of the most powerful country on the planet, we can start to reveal ourselves to the world. Earth is our planet now. You're welcomed to stay and play the part we have chosen for you. Of course, if it's too much for you to handle, we are happy to eliminate you altogether." Vice President Zachary Bradly was emotionless when he spoke.

Her father shot the Bradly a look, then turned back to Fiona. "We have no intention of it coming to that, Fiona. All you have to do is your part, and all will be well."

"We need you with us, dear. You understand, don't you?" Her former mother tilted her head as she always did. Fiona briefly recalled what she looked like as a human. It felt as though spiders were crawling under her skin, unnerving her to the core.

All four aliens were standing side by side, united.

Fiona had no words, so she said nothing.

TO PRESERVE, PROTECT AND DEFEND

{SIX}

THE NEXT DAY, United States President Reid Rockford formally addressed the nation for the first time as President of the United States. Fiona sat to his left and her mother to his right. They listened to his words of wisdom. They smiled as he promised to preserve their nation. They nodded as he agreed to protect each one of them from the evildoers. They held hands as he vowed to defend every human being on the earth to the death.

Then when the cameras shut off, Fiona and her father shared a hug. A hot tear slid down her face.

As she pulled away from the man she called her father, Fiona watched the shadows dance behind the President's eyes seconds before his irises flickered into a slit. Those eyes were the same eyes presiding over her trusting, human nation.

They were the eyes of a monster.

THE END

ABOUT THE AUTHOR

Born and raised in New Jersey, Kristina Rienzi writes suspense thriller fiction. When she's not writing, Kristina enjoys painting, relaxing at the beach, indulging in terrifying entertainment, rooting for the West Virginia University Mountaineers and spending time with her loved ones, wine in hand. She currently lives at the Jersey Shore with her husband, two dogs and cat.

For more information, visit her home on the web:

http://www.KristinaRienzi.com